The Richest Dog on Earth by S. Hopewell
Published by S. Hopewelll
www.shopewellbooks.com

Copyright © 2021 S. Hopewell

All rights reserved. No portion of this book may be reproduced in any form without permission
from the publisher, except as permitted by U.S. copyright law.
For permissions contact: S. Hopewell, smhopewell@outlook.com

Illustrations by H. Oswald and S. Hopewell
ISBN: 978-0-578-95019-8
Printed in USA
First Edition

The Richest Dog on Earth

Written By: S. Hopewell
Pictures By: H. Oswald
and S.Hopewell

Hi!

My name is the Auditor.

 4

I live in a mine yard, on the richest hill on earth.

No one knows why I choose to live here.

8

I do because this place is special to me.

I live alone with no owner to call my own.

The miners make sure to take good care of me.

I never get too close to them.

...But they always leave me plenty of food and water.

They even built me a dog house
to protect me from the weather.

When I vanish for weeks.
They will wonder where I go.

22

I spend my days roaming the hills.

A24

They never know when I will show up again.

26

I come back to them because they are my friends.

I love this place I call home.

Printed in the USA
CPSIA information can be obtained
at www.ICGtesting.com
LVHW070243141024
793737LV00002B/2